Happy Valentine's Day, Mouse!

ISBN 978-0-545-33214-9

12 11 10 9 8 7 6 5 4 3 2   11 12 13 14 15 16/0

Printed in the U.S.A.   40

First Scholastic printing, January 2011

Happy Valentine's Day, Mouse!

Laura Numeroff

Felicia Bond

SCHOLASTIC INC.
New York Toronto London Auckland
dney Mexico City New Delhi Hong Kong

Mouse is making valentines for his friends. He wants each one to be just right.

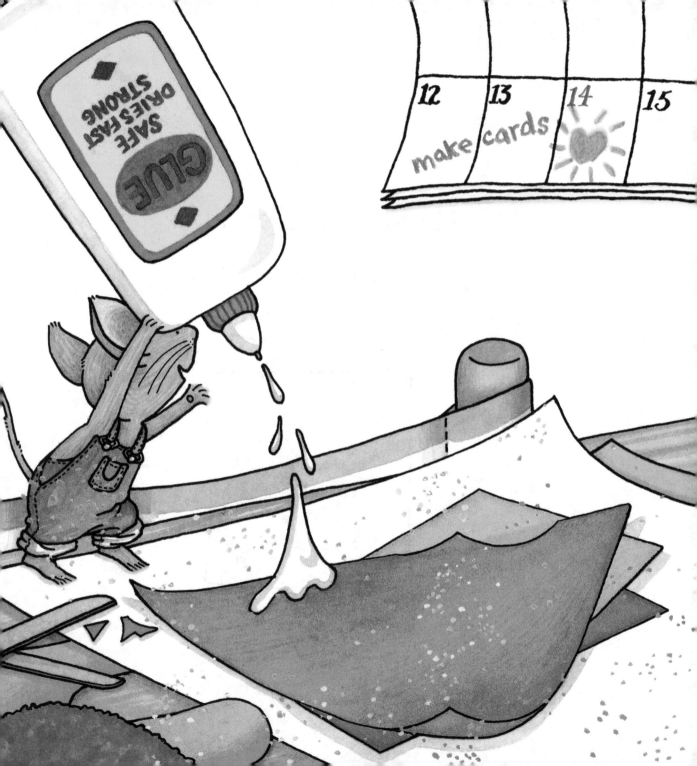

He loves Pig because
she's a good dancer.

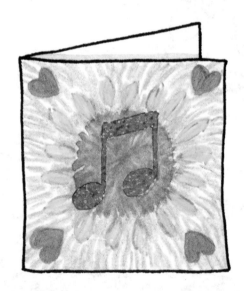

Mouse loves Moose because he's such a good artist.

He loves Cat because
he's so strong . . .

. . . and Dog because he's always happy to see his friends.

He loves Bunny because she's
the best at hide-and-seek . . .

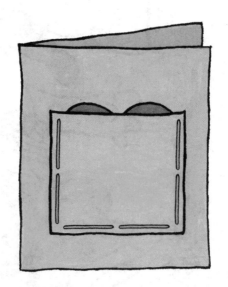

. . . and Fox even though she's not.

Mouse can't wait to give out his valentines.

Who's at the door?

Happy Valentine's Day, Mouse!

For Neil! —F.B.

Happy Valentine's Day to all my friends! —L.N.